KONNECT WITH KIDS

SKIING

THE

# FUNKY DONKEY

## TELLS HIS STORY
## ABOUT HIS

# FIRST
# SKI LESSON

## Herbert K. Naito

**The Funky Donkey Tells His Story About His First Ski Lesson**

iUniverse books may be ordered through booksellers or by contacting:

iUniverse
1663 Liberty Drive
Bloomington, IN 47403
www.iuniverse.com
844-349-9409

Because of the dynamic nature of the Internet, any web addresses or links contained in this book may have changed since publication and may no longer be valid. The views expressed in this work are solely those of the author and do not necessarily reflect the views of the publisher, and the publisher hereby disclaims any responsibility for them.

Any people depicted in stock imagery provided by Getty Images are models, and such images are being used for illustrative purposes only.
Certain stock imagery © Getty Images.

ISBN: 978-1-6632-1325-9 (sc)
ISBN: 978-1-6632-1326-6 (e)

Library of Congress Control Number: 2020922505

Print information available on the last page.

iUniverse rev. date: 12/19/2020

# About the Author

*He spent 40 years in the medical profession. For fun, he coached skiing for over 20 years. He is a member of the Professional Ski Instructors of America and is certified in Alpine Level 2, Children's Specialist Level 2, Adaptive Specialist Level 1, and as a Children's Trainer. Currently he is employed by Vail Ski Resort Management Group and was the former Director of the Children's Advanced Training Specialist, and the Express Pre-School Ski School programs. He is presently on the Vail Ski School Management Group Educational staff.*

# Introduction

Virtually all of the children's comic books on skiing are about entertaining the child; nothing is ever written about SAFETY. There are three factors in the **Professional Ski Motto**: **S**afety, **F**un, and **L**earning. This book not only includes *Entertainment* for the child, but also focuses on ways to ski *Safely*. Many invaluable tips are included on how to go slower and how to follow the safety rules, which are priceless. The *Learning* tips used in this comic book are the same fundamental methods taught at the ski schools by certified children's instructors.

*Wow, it is such a beautiful day…I should go skiing!!! My name is Funky Donkey…*

*What is your name? Do you like to go fast? I do!*

*Wheeeeeeeee, down I go…zoom…*
*Opps…Flop…..Bang…ugh…*

Let's try it again,,,,,Zooom...Wheeeeeee,,,,,,watch out.......out of my way.........Boom...CRASH

The Funky Donkey tries again…zoom…BANG…and crashes into his best friend, Krazy the Kangaroo…BONK! "Hi, I'm Robo the Robot, why don't you take a lesson from a ski instructor?"

*The Funky Donkey quickly replied, "I don't wanna! Nope! Never!*

Hi, Funky Donkey, "I'm your Ski Instructor, Pineapple Herb! Why won't you take a lesson?" Well, let me tell you a short story…My last student refused to take a ski lesson and he was skiing down the hill at a high speed. He couldn't control his speed, nor could he control where his skis were going; he crashed into another person and broke his friend's hands and the other student went to the hospital because he broke his leg and arm."

"Okay, okay, I'll take a ski lesson. I hope that you make it fun and interesting. I sit in a class every day and my teachers are so boring."

Pineapple Herb said, "Congratulations for deciding to take a ski lesson. I will promise to make your lesson full of fun and brief."

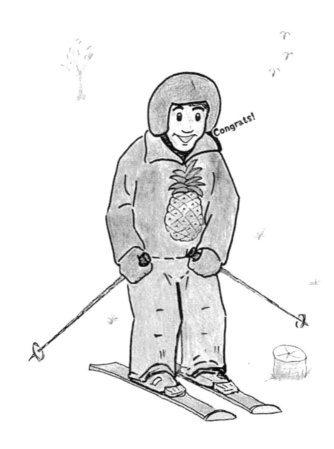

*Funky Donkey, "The first thing you must remember for safety is to ALWAYS wear a helmet…"*

Coach Pineapple Herb is talking to the Funky Donkey, "Going fast on the ski slopes and being out of control is never safe. At first always pick a gentle slope so that you go slower. Never pick a steep slope because you will pick up too much speed. Do you know how to control your speed?" Funky Donkey said, "NO!" Well, Pineapple Herb said that, "there are 4 ways of controlling your speed. First, do not pick a hill that is too steep because you will go too fast and be out of control and get hurt."

Second, "Ski in a wedge, instead of a French Fry. Different size wedges have different speeds. The bigger the wedge, the slower you go; but too big a wedge will cause you to be out-of-balance when you're skiing. Make a medium size wedge; it will be just perfect size (hip width)."

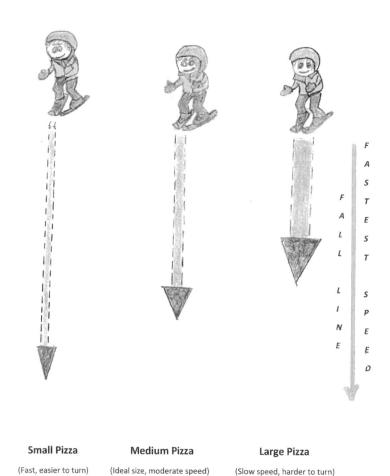

| **Small Pizza** | **Medium Pizza** | **Large Pizza** |
|---|---|---|
| (Fast, easier to turn) | (Ideal size, moderate speed) | (Slow speed, harder to turn) |

Number three, there are 3 types of turn shapes that change the speed when you travel on the skis down the hill. With the J-Turn, you come to a stop after the turn. With the C-Turns, you will slow down after the turn so that you can get ready for the next turn. The S-Turn is the fastest type of turn when going down the hill. The ski Instructor tells the Funky Donkey, *"Don't go straight down in a <u>French Fry;</u> instead I want you to make a J-Turn and come to a complete stop."*

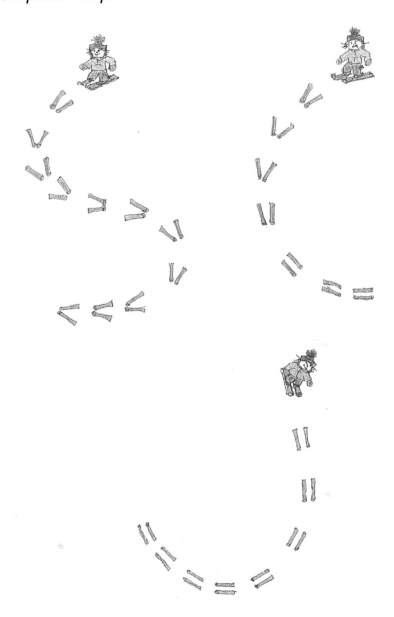

Funky Donkey, now paint the alphabet "J" in the snow with your boot. That's what I want you to do when you're on those skis.'

Now, "Let's ski a series of J-Turns and come to a complete stop. Let's try that again and wait longer, and longer before you make your turns. So, you can go faster and faster down the hill, but you can always bail out of the speed by making a turn and going uphill to stop (a J-Turn). With this turn, you shouldn't be afraid of too much speed because you know how to bail out."

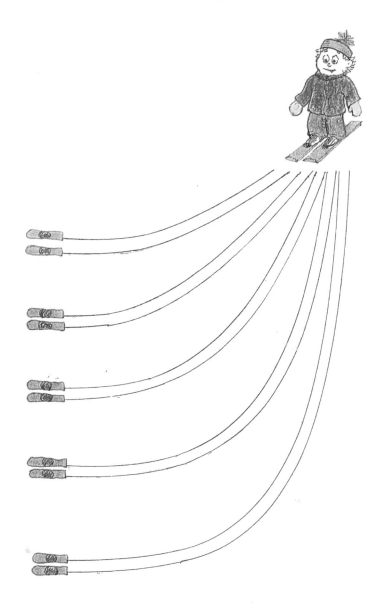

*"Now paint the alphabet 'C' in the snow with your boot.*

*Now, Let's make C-Turns so can make the turns going at a slower speed.*

*Now, when you're going down the hill too fast, turn quickly and go to the side of the hill to slow down or go up the hill if you want to stop."*

*Remember Funky Donkey, the fourth method of going slower is "the <u>Pizza way</u>, which is always the slower way to go rather than French Fry way and make a lot of turns. The more turns that you make, the slower you go.*

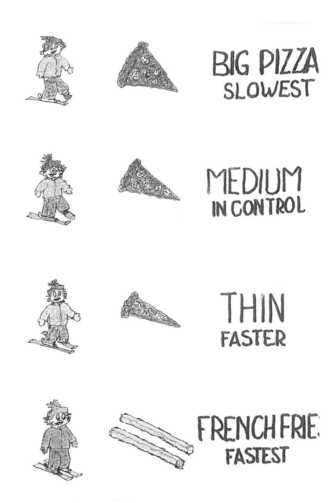

BIG PIZZA
SLOWEST

MEDIUM
IN CONTROL

THIN
FASTER

FRENCH FRIE:
FASTEST

When you get better with the wedge-Turns, I will teach you French-Fry Turns."

*Now, let's meet your friend, Wacky Dog. You can tell him how much safety you have learned. Also, always remember that the skier in front of you must always be avoided so that they don't get hurt. For the skiers behind you or above you, you must watch out for them so that they don't bang into you. Thus, always look around before you start down the hill."*

*"Now, lets let's ski down the hill by connecting all your turns going down the hill to greet your friend Wacky Dog and tell him all the things that you have learned."*

So, Pineapple Herb asks Funky Donkey," what did you learn today?" Funky said, "I learned that:

- I must always wear a helmet to protect my precious brain
- Going fast is dangerous and could hurt someone or myself
- Zooming straight down the hill can cause a crash that could hurt me
- Going slower is always more fun and is safer
- Making J-Turns make you stop; and C-Turns make you go slower
- Skiing in a Pizza also makes me go slower than in French Fries
- Compared to "J-Turns" and "C-Turns", "S-Turns" are faster
- Always watch for the person in front of you, and the person skiing above or behind you; they have the right-of-way (you should not go until the coast is clear). "

Your other good friend, Grumpy Bear, is waiting for you at the bottom of the other hill and is anxious to hear from you. He is no longer grumpy because he was told that Pineapple Herb taught Funky Donkey all about skiing safety and about staying in BALANCE so that you don't have to fall and crash all the time. It makes Grumpy Bear so, so happy that you won't get hurt while skiing and how much fun you had.

Funky Donkey, told Grumpy Bear that, "Besides knowing how to turn slowly in control, the coach reminded me that, *I must remain balanced throughout each of the turns.*" How do you do that? Well, Pineapple Herb said, *"To always have your knees ahead of your toes, and your nose ahead of your knees with your hands forward at all times. To help get your nose forward, bend from the waist (hips) like you're bowing down. Whenever I sit back, I will fall. When my mom or dad drives the car, they sit in the front sit; so, for me to drive my skis, I need to stand in the front seat of the skis (where my feet are). My body needs to be balanced right over my feet"*

*We played a game for BALANCE. Pineapple Herb put a $100 in my boot between my shin and tongue of the boot. He said to press the $100 so my knees come forward. Bend a little bit at the hips so that my nose come forward too. My knees and nose forward will help me so that I'm in better balance on my feet.*

*"Funky Donkey, I'm so proud of you because you learned to ski slowly and safely and in balance. Coach Pineapple Herb is going to give you a Special Award for Safety"*

*Notice the three people are skiing safely and in balance.*

*'A Funky Donkey that skis SAFELY is a happy Donkey'*

Printed in the United States
By Bookmasters